RUDAS

NIÑO'S HORRENDOUS
HERMANITAS

TÉCNICOS
TEC-nee-kohs

"Good guys" who play by the rules

EL EXTRATERRESTRE

CABEZA OLMECA

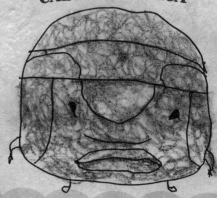

RUDOS
ROO-dohs

"Tough guys" who bend or break the rules

NIÑO

LAS HERMANITAS

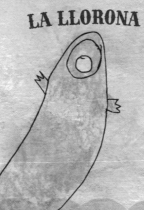

LA LLORONA

LA MOMIA DE GUANAJUATO

EL CHAMUCO

Match dedicated to

Moni Blast and Octavio el Dialéctico de la Justicia

SQUARE
FISH

An imprint of Macmillan Publishing Group, LLC
175 Fifth Avenue, New York, NY 10010
mackids.com

Square Fish and the Square Fish logo are trademarks of Macmillan and are used by Roaring Brook Press under license from Macmillan.

Our books may be purchased in bulk for promotional, educational, or business use. Please contact your local bookseller or the Macmillan
Corporate and Premium Sales Department at (800) 221-7945 ext. 5442 or by e-mail at MacmillanSpecialMarkets@macmillan.com.

Library of Congress Cataloging-in-Publication Data

Names: Morales, Yuyi, author.
Title: Rudas: Niño's horrendous hermanitas / Yuyi Morales.
Description: New York : Roaring Brook Press, 2016. | "A Neal
  Porter Book." | Summary: "Niño's little sisters get in on the wrestling
  action"— Provided by publisher.
Identifiers: LCCN 2016004882 | ISBN 978-1-250-14336-5 (paperback)
Subjects: | CYAC: Wrestling—Fiction. | Brothers and sisters—Fiction. |
  BISAC: JUVENILE FICTION / Sports & Recreation / Wrestling. | JUVENILE
  FICTION / People & Places / United States / Hispanic & Latino. | JUVENILE
  FICTION / Family / Siblings.
Classification: LCC PZ7.M7881927 Ru 2016 | DDC [E]—dc23
LC record available at https://lccn.loc.gov/2016004882

Originally published in the United States
by Neal Porter Books/Roaring Brook Press
First Square Fish edition, 2018
Book designed by Andrew Arnold
Square Fish logo designed by Filomena Tuosto

3 5 7 9 10 8 6 4

RUDAS

~NIÑO'S HORRENDOUS HERMANITAS

YUYI MORALES

SQUARE
FISH

A NEAL PORTER BOOK
ROARING BROOK PRESS
NEW YORK

Everybody was minding their own business when . . .

SEÑORAS Y SEÑORES NIÑOS Y NIÑAS

The time has come to welcome the phenomenal, spectacular, legendary ne of a kind . . .

¡LAS HERMANITAS!

Wrestling champions!
Lucha Queens!

The little sisters reign supreme, cracking down on their opponents with incredibly rude feats.

Watch out, here comes
their first one!
BOOM, BOOM, BOOM!
The Poopy Bomb Blowout!

Such a rotten move!

In no time the **EL EXTRATERRESTRE**
is gassed out of this world!

CABEZA OLMECA is up next with his best Diaper Change, but no one expected Las Hermanitas' famous Nappy Freedom Break so early in the match!

Cabeza Olmeca's head is stunned!

EL CHAMUCO didn't see
their next hideous move coming.

Tag Team Teething is Las Hermanitas' hot ticket to doom!

Preposterous!
Las Hermanitas escape
from dire straits
with the Twofer Tattle!

¡Madre!
Will anyone be spared
from their Pampered
Plunder?

But wait. What is that?

It is . . .

. . . a Look-and-Book Diversion. And they fell for it!
Unbelievable!

ZZZÁCATELAS

Such a brotherly trick!

How will Las Hermanitas handle
this heartbreaking breakout?

Nothing this juicy has happened since last season's Great Lemon Squirt.

What a wretched turn of events.
Not to mention twice as loud.

Can anyone make them stop already?

What a Seize and Squeeze!
¡Sí, Señor!

Las Hermanitas' strong hold is inescapable!
They are

RUDAS!

LUCHA RIMBOMBANTE
LOO-cha Reem-bohm-BAN-teh

★ ★ ★

Spectacular battle

MUY CARO
Moo-ee KAH-ro

★ ★ ★

Very expensive

SANTOS PAÑALES
SAHN-tohs Pah-NYAH-lehs

★ ★ ★

Holy diapers

MÍO
MEE-oh

★ ★ ★

Mine

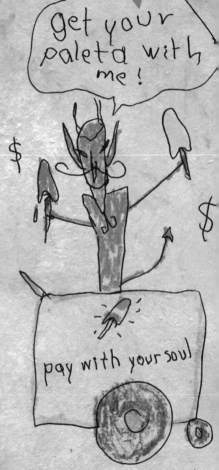

MIS HIJOS
Mees EE-hohs
★ ★ ★
My children

MAROMAS VOLADORAS
Mah-ROH-mahs
Voh-lah-doh-rahs
★ ★ ★
Flying somersaults

FUEGO EN EL CUADRILÁTERO
FOOEH-geoh ehn el
kwah-dree-LAH-tehr-oh
★ ★ ★
Fire in the ring